STOP!

For
Matt & Sarah,
Rosie & Will,
with love
—J.L.

To Tamar & Eve,
Astrid & Doogie, Joel,
big Eve, Ben & Simon,
Greta & Marco—
who have not read this book!
—D.A.

tiger tales
an imprint of ME Media, LLC
202 Old Ridgefield Road, Wilton, CT 06897
Published in the United States 2010
Originally published in Great Britain 2009
by Egmont UK Limited
Text copyright ©2009 Jill Lewis
Illustrations copyright ©2009 Deborah Allwright
CIP data is available
ISBN-13: 978-1-58925-094-9
ISBN-10: 1-58925-094-X
Printed in Singapore
TWP0110
For more insight and activities, visit us at www.tigertalesbooks.com

Th **DON'T** **READ** **THIS** **BOOK!**

by

Jill Lewis

Illustrated by
Deborah
Allwright

tiger tales

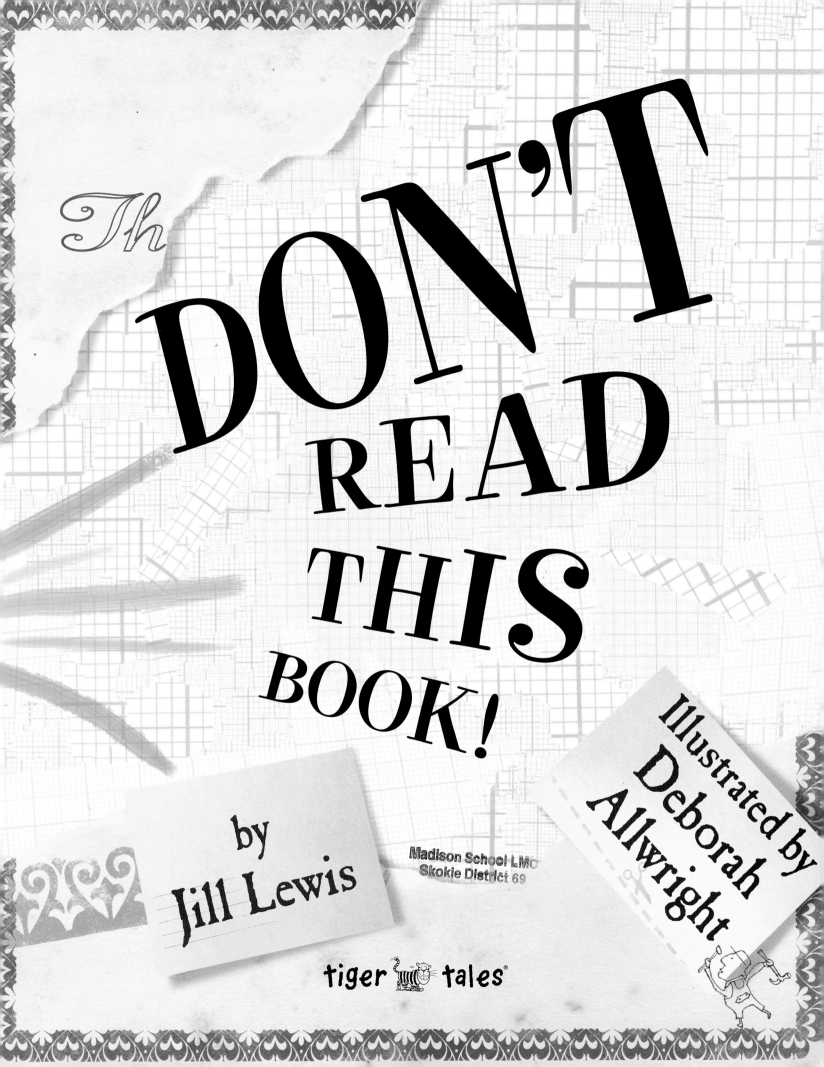

Once
upon
a time,

on a dark
and stormy
night, a

STOP RIGHT THERE!

Once upon a time, absolutely nothing happened whatsoever! I command you to go and read something else! There is no story here.

But someone had started reading now, hadn't they? (Yes, I do mean YOU.)

The King called his story writer.

What do you mean it's not ready? I was promised a new story and a new story I shall have.

The King needed to find his story writer fast because he had the feeling he was being watched....

You again! Go away or I'll fling you in prison!

That's crumby!

The King met his story writer.

Ah, there you are. My new story is supposed to be starting right **this minute!** **Where is it?**

Er . . . I had some notes, but I've . . . er . . . lost them. I do have the title, Sire. Well, **half** the title. I had it on this piece of paper here, you see, but it's . . . um . . . torn.

The Princess and the . . . something. What kind of a title is that? **Where** can we find the **rest** of it?

The story writer thought hard.

Well, I've just come back from Beanstalk Crossroads. It might be there.

What are we waiting for?

Let's go find it.

On the way to Beanstalk Crossroads, the King and the story writer tried desperately to think of the title.

Was it The Princess and the **Incredibly Handsome King?**

Er . . . No.

Was it The Princess and the **Amazingly Wise King?**

Er . . . No.

Was it The Princess and the **Unbelievably Brave King?**

No, Sire.
Sorry, Sire.

While they were thinking, a certain someone was still reading.

(Yes, I do mean YOU.)

page of this book

OW YOU IN DUNGEON!

Can't you see there's no story? GO away!

No, wait a minute!

The story begins with <u>a storm</u>.

Good. I like a bit of **drama**.

And then there's this <u>**princess**</u>.

I think we'd guessed that on our own. Any other characters like a handsome, brave, and smart **king**, for instance?

Oh yes, <u>Your Majesty</u>.

There's definitely <u>a **king** in this story</u>.

Well, it wouldn't be a good story without one. So, what's going to **happen**?

The writer looked around him.
There were no more pages.
What was he going to do?

IS THIS WHAT YOU'RE LOOKING FOR?

The next two pages! Yippee!

We need...let me see...

a queen and a prince and

fifteen mattresses

and a...

They raced to Grandma's cottage...
where they thoroughly confused
the Wolf.

Er...my, my,
Your Majesty,
What fine clothes you have!
What fancy shoes you have!
What a big crown
you have...

Yes, yes, that's enough of that!

We need your mattresses and we need them now. Get out of bed **immediately.**

Suddenly, the writer came running in.

I've found my notes! We just need one more thing...

I thought you were never

So now we've got everything. We've got all the **characters** and the **beginning** and the **middle** and the **end**!

This is so **exciting**!

It's fantastic, it's...

Wait.

Oh, be quiet. Look! We've run out of space!

We can't tell the story anyway. I am not pleased!

P

And we STILL don't EVEN have the title.

I have an idea.

We can tell it on the last pages.

But we'll have to be really quick.

Oh, and the title.

I've found that, too.

It's . . .

O

ND!

The Princess

Once upon a time, on a dark and stormy night, a princess traveled through wind and rain to reach the castle of her beloved but because of the storm the King (who incidentally was both handsome and brave)

and the Queen of the castle did not believe that such a wet and messy girl could really be a princess.

So the Queen (having taken the advice of her very wise and good-looking husband) decided to give her a test so she asked the

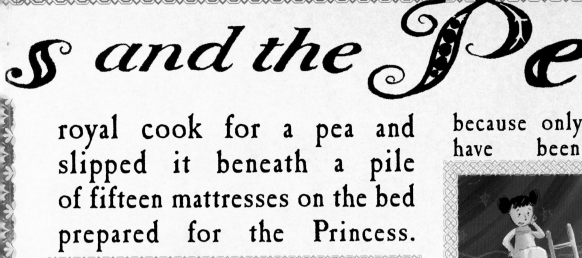

royal cook for a pea and slipped it beneath a pile of fifteen mattresses on the bed prepared for the Princess.

because only a princess could have been so delicate.

On hearing the good news the Prince immediately proposed to the Princess,

When the next morning the Princess complained that she hadn't slept a wink because of the lump in her bed both the Queen and the King (whose **cunning** and **brilliant** plan had clearly worked) knew she must really be a princess

and the Prince and the Princess were married andtheyalllivedhappilyeverafterTHE END!

phew!

WHAT, ARE YOU STILL HERE?

It's your bedtime!

Go away.

And don't you dare read this book again!